Dear r

Welcome to the world of

Geronimo Stilton

MINI MYSTERY 5

THE RODENT'S GAZETTE
EDITORIAL STAFF

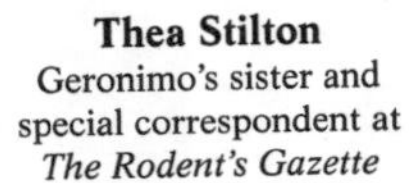

Geronimo Stilton
A learned and brainy
mouse; editor of
The Rodent's Gazette

Thea Stilton
Geronimo's sister and
special correspondent at
The Rodent's Gazette

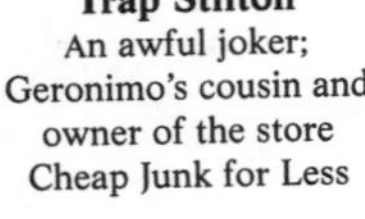

Trap Stilton
An awful joker;
Geronimo's cousin and
owner of the store
Cheap Junk for Less

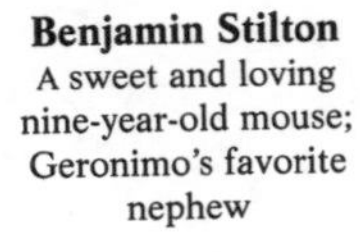

Benjamin Stilton
A sweet and loving
nine-year-old mouse;
Geronimo's favorite
nephew

Geronimo Stilton

THE DOUBLE CROSS

Scholastic Inc.

ISBN 978-0-545-64289-7

Based on an original idea by Elisabetta Dami.
www.geronimostilton.com

Published by Scholastic Inc., 557 Broadway, New York, NY 10012.

Text by Geronimo Stilton
Original title *La doppia ladra*
Cover by Giuseppe Ferrario and Giulia Zaffaroni
Illustrations by Elena Tomasutti (pencils and inks) and Davide Turotti (color)
Graphics by Michela Battaglin and Marta Lorini

Special thanks to Kathryn Cristaldi
Translated by Andrea Schaffer
Interior design by Becky James

Fingerprint on cover and page i © NREY/Shutterstock

First printing, June 2014 by Scholastic Malaysia, operating under Grolier (Malaysia) Sdn. Bhd.

Printed in Malaysia

A Simple Electric Razor!

What was I doing on a cruise ship? It made no sense. I don't like boats or big waves, and I almost always get **seasick**. . . .

Well, it all started when my electric razor broke. One morning I turned on my RAZOR to shave and KAPOW! Just like that, my razor practically EXPLODED in my paws, burning off half my fur!

I couldn't go to work in that state, so . . .

Oops! What a scatterbrain . . . I forgot to introduce myself. My name is Stilton, *Geronimo Stilton*. I run *The Rodent's Gazette*, the most famouse newspaper on Mouse Island.

Anyway, as I was saying, I couldn't go to work with fried fur, so I scampered off to the electronics store **Wired Whiskers** to buy a new razor.

"I need an electric razor," I told the salesmouse.

"Awesome!" he squeaked. "This week we're having lots of **SPECIALS**!"

He opened up a glass case filled with razors.

"You see this one?" he asked. "While you shave, you can listen to your favorite music. And it comes with a free pair of GLOW-IN-THE-DARK slippers!"

"But I don't need slippers," I protested.

"Then how about this one," he went on, holding up a razor that glittered. "Those are genuine diamonds!"

I almost choked when I saw the price.

"It comes with a free ten-year supply of spicy cheeses!" the salesmouse chirped.

"But I don't like spicy cheeses," I said.

"Well, here's one that comes with a SOLAR-POWERED lawn mower!" offered the salesmouse.

Finally, I couldn't take it anymore. "I just want a normal PLASTIC razor!" I whined.

The salesmouse looked surprised. "Why didn't you say so?" he squeaked. "Here's the one you want. It's the Goodfur plastic razor. It comes with a chance to win a cruise to the Caribbean!"

I bought the razor. As for the cruise, I never gave it a second thought.

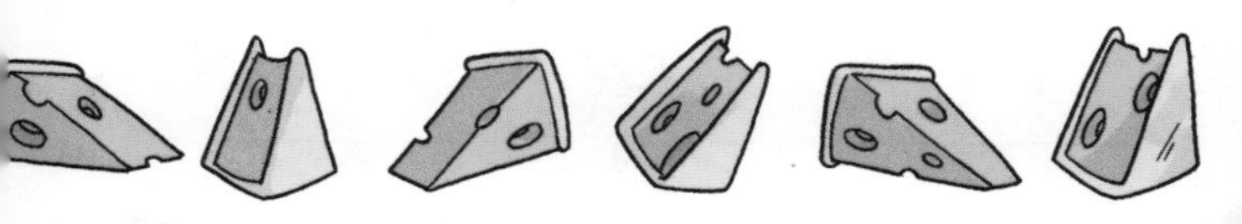

Two weeks later, a registered letter arrived for me:

> **CONGRATULATIONS!**
>
> You are the **lucky** winner of an all-expense-paid, **six**-day, **seven**-night cruise to the Caribbean for **four rodents**!
>
> *Brought to you by the fine rodents at Goodfur!*

I sighed. As I mentioned, I'm not cruise mouse material. Just the thought of being on a boat for six days and seven nights made me feel **seasick**. But suddenly, I had an **idea**.

YOU CAN DO IT!

What if I were to invite Petunia Pretty Paws? Ah, what a fascinating rodent! I have had a huge crush on Petunia for the longest time. Maybe if I took her on the cruise, it wouldn't be so awful. If only I could muster the courage to call her. Oh, why am I so shy around Petunia?

You can do it! I told myself as I reached for the phone. And just then, the phone rang.

The voice on the other end of the line made my heart melt.

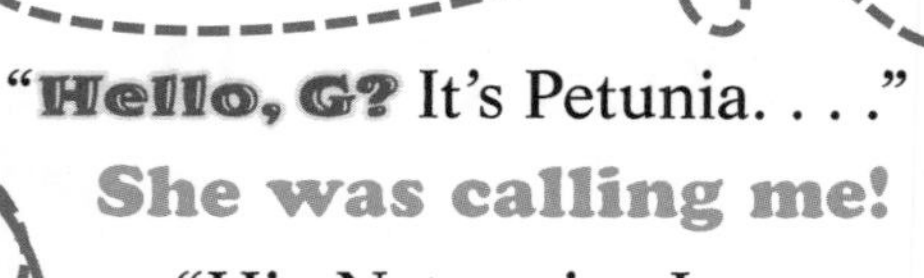

"Hello, G? It's Petunia. . . ."

She was calling me!

"Hi, Netpunia, I mean, Tepunia, I mean, Petunia," I babbled. Oh, how **embarrassing**!

Luckily, Petunia didn't seem to notice. "I was hoping you could help me, G," she went on. "The government of **New Zealand** has asked me to make a documentary on the endangered **kiwi** bird. It would be an **amazing** opportunity for me."

"Congratulations!" I squeaked.

"Thanks!" Petunia

KIWI

It's the national bird of New Zealand. It has a very long beak and very small wings, but it cannot fly. It is shy and nocturnal, and it eats small insects, seeds, and worms.

gushed. "There's only one problem. Could you watch my niece Bugsy Wugsy for a few days? What do you say, G?"

I have to admit, Bugsy can really get under my fur at times. But I would never say no to Petunia, so I agreed. Then I had another idea. I could invite Bugsy, Benjamin, and my sister, Thea, to come on the cruise with me.

"Oh, G, you're the best!" exclaimed Petunia. "Bugsy will be so excited!"

I hung up the phone with a smile on my face. I **LOVE** making Petunia happy. Too bad she wouldn't be with me on the cruise. I could just picture it: me, the mouse of my **dreams**, the **sunset**, the sea . . . Oh, well. Maybe next time!

EIGHT ON THE DOT

The following morning we met at **EIGHT ON THE DOT**. Thea pulled up in her **RED** sports car with Benjamin and Bugsy in the backseat.

"Thanks for the invitation, Gerry Berry!" my sister said. "I really needed a nice vacation."

"I've never been on a **Caribbean** cruise before!" squeaked my nephew. "Thanks, Uncle Geronimo!"

Next to Benjamin, Bugsy was jumping **UP** and **DOWN** as if her fur were on fire.

"This is Sooo awesome, Uncle G!" she shrieked.

"Awesome," I agreed. Yes, a relaxing vacation *would* be awesome, if only I could forget about . . .

. . . the seasickness

. . . the big waves

. . . the too-hard or too-soft mattress

. . . the rodent-eating sharks

. . . the ship sinking

. . . the too-cold nights

. . . the burning sun

. . . the mosquitoes

. . . the pooping seagulls

. . . and worst of all, the homesickness.

Yep, I'd *just* have to forget those things. But how?

The *Queen Cheesy II*

Twenty minutes later, we reached the port of New Mouse City ready to board the cruise ship, the **Queen Cheesy II**.

Slimy Swiss rolls! That boat was enormouse!

A rodent welcomed us to the ship.

"You must be the winners of the **Goodfur** vacation," he said. "I'm Captain Rolando Squeakando. Welcome!"

"Excuse me, Captain, how many **LIFEBOATS** are there on the **Queen Cheesy II**?" I asked.

The captain looked at me sharply. "Are you suggesting my ship is not **SAFE**, Mr. Stilton?" he asked.

Uh-oh. We hadn't even set sail and I had already insulted the mouse in charge.

"N-no, sorry," I stammered. "I just get worried."

"Well, don't worry!" Squeakando replied confidently. "We have LIFEBOATS and LIFE VESTS for every passenger!"

I must admit I was relieved. And I was glad I had put four life vests in my suitcase, just in case. Better SAFE than sorry!

Inflate Slowly . . . or Else!

All of our cabins were on the top level, which was called the **Sky Deck**.

I found an enormouse box in my cabin. A label on the side read: “Use in case of emergency!”

How strange! The writing looked so familiar. Inside the box I found a **yellow** life vest and a **yellow** hat.

How strange! That hat reminded me of someone, but I couldn’t remember who. A card attached to the vest read: **“INFLATE SLOWLY . . . OR ELSE!”**

How strange! I wondered what

that meant. I decided there was only one way to find out. Even though it wasn't an emergency, I picked up the vest and began to INFLATE it slowly.

As I was blowing, I heard laughter.

HEE! HEE! HEE!

How strange! I was the only one in the cabin!

I kept blowing. Again, it sounded as if someone was laughing.

HEE! HEE! HEE!

My head began to pound. My fur stood on end. Who cares about getting seasick! Now I was worried about a ghost! Was my cabin haunted?

I was so nervous, I started blowing really fast.

Just then, there was a loud BOOM!

Suddenly, a mouse stood before me wearing a yellow hat and a yellow raincoat.

"How did you like my little joke, Geronimo?" he asked.

It was my friend the famouse detective **Hercule Poirat**.

"Hercule, I didn't know you were on this cruise!" I squeaked.

"Yep, I'm on the floor right below you, the Empress Deck," he said. "And I see you are traveling with the lovely Thea. Can I sit with you at dinner?"

Hercule has a crush on my sister even though she never gives him the TIME of day.

Still, I nodded **YES**. What else could I say?

A Cloud of Perfume

At dinnertime, the restaurant was full of mice.

I spotted Hercule over at the buffet, piling his plate SKY-HIGH with delicious-looking cheese appetizers.

Then I headed to my table, where Thea, Bugsy, and Benjamin were waiting for me. But before I reached them, I collided with a lady rodent who had dropped her evening bag.

I bent down to get it for her and was wrapped up in a cloud of perfume!

The smell was so strong, I got **dizzy** and crashed into a waiter carrying a pot of something **steaming**.

Oh, how **embarrassing**!

"I-I'm S-S-orry!" I stammered, struggling to get up.

She looked at me and I nearly fainted. Her CLEAR BLUE eyes were the color of a gorgeous summer sky and her fur was so **shiny**. What a rodent!

"Don't worry, Mr. Stilton, everyone knows great writers get distracted," she said in a voice as sweet as honey.

"You know me?" I squeaked.

She flashed me a charming smile. "But of course! I am Lily Lovelyfur, one of your biggest fans!" she crooned.

I **blushed**. Then I watched in a daze while she joined our table.

Lily Lovelyfur

Would You Like to Dance?

Lily Lovelyfur was mesmerizing. And best of all, she seemed to be interested in me! I was so thrilled I hardly touched my food.

"Aren't you hungry, Uncle Geronimo?" Benjamin asked.

"Maybe he's SEASICK," Bugsy suggested.

Thea caught me staring at Lily Lovelyfur and grinned. "Or maybe he's got a little crush on a certain mouse," she teased in a singsong voice.

Before I could protest, the captain

stood up. "I'd like to welcome everyone aboard the **Queen Cheesy II**. Here's to a fabumouse voyage! And now it is our tradition to begin our cruise with some **paw-tapping** ballroom dancing!"

Within seconds, a distinguished-looking mouse appeared at our table.

"I am **Count Richie Richpaws**. May I have this dance?" he asked Thea.

"Certainly, Count," she accepted with a smile.

I wasn't surprised. My sister loves a **dashing** mouse who can dance!

"Richie Richpaws," Hercule

scoffed. "What a ridiculous name."

I was about to offer Hercule my cheddar roll to cheer him up when Miss Lovelyfur squeaked, "How about you, Mr. Stilton? Would you like to dance with me?"

Would I?! Does a mouse have whiskers?!

I jumped to my paws so fast I nearly fell flat on my snout.

But just as we started to dance, a mouse scampered into the ballroom.

"HELP! HELP!" she squeaked. "There's a THIEF on this ship!"

Help! Help!

A Thief in the Night!

It was Countess Von Mousenschnitz.

Sobbing, she explained how she had returned to her cabin on the Sky Deck and discovered the porthole open and her jewelry box empty!

The captain questioned all of the passengers but he didn't uncover any CLUES.

Lily grabbed my paw. "Good thing we were together, Mr. Stilton," she squeaked. "Otherwise we might have been SUSPECTS."

I was less worried about being a suspect and more worried about being robbed myself. What if a thief stole my WHISKER TRIMMER or my GLOW-IN-THE-DARK flashlight? They weren't worth a lot of MONEY, but they were important to me.

Of course, I tried to act Brave for Lily. She agreed to let me accompany her to her cabin, which was on the Empress Deck, the floor below mine.

"What a gentlemouse," she cooed.

But when we arrived, she quickly slammed the door in my snout!

How strange!

And before she slammed the door, I noticed something odd inside her cabin.

CLUE 1

Can you spot something odd in Lily Lovelyfur's cabin?

We Smell a Rat!

I headed up to the Sky Deck, still thinking about the mysterious shadow I had seen on the wall in Lily Lovelyfur's cabin. What did it mean?

I was so deep in thought I ran right into a group of rodents.

OOOF!

Luckily, it was my family.

"We were just looking for you, Uncle Geronimo," Benjamin said. "We smell a rat!"

"I think we need to investigate this THEFT," Hercule explained.

We went right to Countess Von Mousenschnitz's cabin. She showed us the empty jewelry box and the small porthole the thief had used.

Hercule pulled out a measuring tape. "This porthole is only one foot wide. It must have been a very THIN thief . . . or maybe a mouselet."

"I haven't seen any mouselets on board except for Bugsy and Benjamin," Thea said.

"And I haven't noticed any extremely THIN mice on board, either," Hercule added.

Suddenly, a TERRIFYING thought hit me. What if there really was a ghost on the ship? Could a ghost be responsible for the missing jewelry on the Queen Cheesy II?

I was about to squeak up when Thea looked out the porthole.

"Hey, there's a rope DANGLING out here," she said. "The thief must have used it to climb down from the Sky

Deck to the Empress Deck."

Meanwhile, Bugsy picked something up off the carpet. "Look, everyone!" she squeaked. "It's a **BLUE** contact lens!"

The countess quickly assured us the **contact lens** did not belong to her.

"Now we know something more about the **THIEF**!" Benjamin declared.

CLUE 2

What do we know now about the mysterious thief?

Huh?

The next morning on my way to breakfast I saw Lily Lovelyfur. She was wearing big, **DARK** sunglasses.

"Good morning, Miss Furrylove . . . I mean, Miss Loveydove . . . I mean . . ." I stammered.

"Good morning, Mr. Stilton!" she **interrupted** me. She smiled. "I **love** cruises, don't you? I'm going to the pool to get some **sun**."

After breakfast I returned to my CABIN. On the way there, I ran into Miss Lovelyfur again.

How strange!

"I thought you were going to the POOL," I said.

"Oh, no, Mr. Stilton," she replied. "It's too early for the POOL. First I need a nice breakfast."

She gave me a little wave and disappeared. I stared after her, confused. Was I losing my marbles? I decided I needed some fresh air.

I scampered to the upper deck. It really was a **beautiful** day. The sun was **shining** and a gentle **wind** was blowing. And for once, I didn't feel seasick!

Absentmindedly, I wandered over to the pool, where I found Miss Lovelyfur sunbathing!

"Oh, Mr. Stilton, I can't wait to root for you in the **diving competition** at the pool," she squeaked. "Your friend Hercule said you had signed up."

HUH? Now I was more confused than ever!

What was going on with Miss Lovelyfur? And what diving competition was she squeaking about?

I went downstairs to ask Hercule and ran into Miss Lovelyfur . . . again!

"Time for some sun," she said.

My head was spinning.

CLUE 3

What did Geronimo Stilton see that was so strange?

I Don't Know How to Dive!

Before I could discuss things with Hercule, he grabbed my paw.

"You need an energy-packed breakfast if you're going to compete in the **diving competition**," he said. Then he made me eat:

4 hot chocolates with extra cream

1 supersized banana smoothie

"But I already ate breakfast!" I protested. "And I don't even know how to dive!"

"Oh, don't be silly, Geronimo. You can do it!" Hercule insisted.

Then he dragged me to his cabin and made me change into a bright yellow bathing suit with BANANAS all over it. I looked ridiculous! How embarrassing!

Don't Look Down!

All of the passengers had gathered on the pool deck to watch the competition.

The captain spoke from a megaphone:

"Ladies and gentlemice, welcome to the *Queen Cheesy II's* fabumouse diving competition!"

I **trembled** with fear. The diving board was so **HIGH**! I wondered if I would even be able to make it up the ladder! I thought about ***running*** away.

But when I looked around, I saw Benjamin, Bugsy, Thea, and even **Count Richie Richpaws** all cheering me on.

What could I do? I couldn't disappoint everyone. When it was my turn, I slowly began **CLIMBING** up the ladder.

Holey cheese! I was so dizzy from the HEIGHT!

I glanced down and spotted Lily Lovelyfur. She blew me a kiss! Now I felt even dizzier!

"Don't look down!" I heard Hercule shout from below.

Don't look down! I thought to myself as I walked to the edge of the board.

Little did I know, Hercule had put a banana peel on the diving board! Suddenly, I slipped, BOUNCED, did three spectacular somersaults, and fell snoutfirst into the water.

It was a perfect dive!

When I emerged from the water, everyone was applauding!

I had **WON**!

Eyes Like Green Emeralds!

That night, there was an AWARDS CEREMONY.

"I told you you could do it!" Hercule said, shaking my paw until I felt like it would fall off.

"You could have killed me with that BANANA PEEL," I muttered.

But Hercule just winked.

Meanwhile, Benjamin, Bugsy, Thea, and Count Richpaws all congratulated me.

"Way to go, Uncle Geronimo!" my nephew squeaked.

"I thought you'd **CRACK** your head

open like a nut, Uncle G!" Bugsy marveled.

"It would be my **pleasure** if you would join me tonight at my table, Mr. Stilton," the count declared. "And why don't you ask your friend Miss Lovelyfur to join us, too?"

Suddenly, Lily appeared by my side. Before I could even squeak a word, she said, "I would **love** to join you, Mr. Stilton. Who wouldn't want to have dinner with such a talented **ATHLETE**?!"

She lowered her glasses and winked at me. Then she scampered off.

I stood there, **dazzled** by her

eyes, which sparkled like **green emeralds**!

A funny feeling came over me. There was something different about Miss Lovelyfur, but I just couldn't put my paw on it. Did she have a new **fur-style**? Was she wearing a different shade of **lipstick**?

It was all so confusing. I was still

thinking about Lily when the count cleared his throat.

"See you at dinner, Mr. Stilton. And now, I promised your sister I would show her one of my most **priceless** collections."

After they left, Benjamin **TUGGED** on my sleeve. "Uncle Geronimo, did you notice something different about Miss Lovelyfur?" he squeaked. "Something about her eyes?"

Just then it **hit** me! Now I knew exactly what was different!

CLUE 4

What do Benjamin and Geronimo realize is different about Lily Lovelyfur?

Sorry I'm Late!

At dinner, we all sat at the count's table. The waiters began serving our meal, but still there was no SIGN of Lily. Was she SICK? Was it something I said?

But then suddenly Lily appeared. Once again, I was **dazzled** by her eyes. But this time they were **BLUE** again!

How strange! This afternoon I was sure her eyes had been **green**. I made a mental note to make an appointment with my eye doctor, Dr. Bifocals, when I

got home. Maybe I was colorblind!

"Good evening, everyone. Sorry I'm late!" Miss Lovelyfur apologized. "I was feeling a little SEASICK. I don't like cruises very much."

Huh? Now I was really confused. That didn't make sense.

But before I had a chance to ask, THREE things happened. First, Hercule accidentally squeezed lemon juice in my eye. Next, he ladled a spoonful of boiling soup on my paw by mistake. And finally, he HIT ME in the snout with a piece of cake! I WAS A MESS!

I was hoping no one had noticed when the count suggested we all go

Hercule sprayed lemon juice in my eye.

He spilled boiling soup on my paw.

Then he flung a piece of cake on my snout.

outside to look at the STARS.

"I need to grab something from my cabin, then I'll meet you," he said.

The rest of us headed up to the deck. It was a beautiful night. The sea was calm, there was a cool breeze, and the stars twinkled overhead.

The smell of Lily's perfume made me smile.

Still, I couldn't stop thinking about what she had said. . . .

CLUE 5

What did Lily say that didn't make any sense?

What a beautiful sky!
Wow!

THIEF! THIEF!

I was still thinking about Lily when suddenly we heard a mouse squeaking in the ballroom.

"THIEF! THIEF! My gold watches are gone!"

We dashed inside and discovered the count in a RAGE.

"It was you!" he squeaked, pointing at Thea. "I showed you my precious collection of gold watches, and then you stole them!"

Thea **narrowed** her eyes. Uh-oh. I

could tell she was ANGRIER than a lab rat stuck in a maze!

"How dare you accuse me!" she squeaked, her eyes **flashing**.

One thing you should know about Thea is that she is one **TOUGH** mouse. Her paws were **balled** into fists. She

looked like she wanted to **SHOUT** right back at Count Richie.

Luckily, the **captain** arrived.

"Calm down, everyone," he said, holding up a paw. "Tell me what happened. . . ."

Before the count could explain, my sister **blurted** out the whole story. I confirmed that Thea had been with us the whole time, so she couldn't be the **THIEF**. The captain agreed.

"Don't worry," he said. "We will **MONITOR** the cabins day and night until we catch the thief.

You have my **WORD**!"

We left the ballroom and returned to our cabins for the night. Before I reached mine, though, I decided to do the gentlemousely thing and walk Lily back to her cabin.

She thanked me with a **mesmerizing** smile. Ah, what a mouse. "I'm so glad I was with you, Mr. Stilton," she squeaked. "I would hate it if anyone thought we were **suspects**."

I left her at her door and returned to my cabin. Later, I was just drifting off to sleep when there was a knock at my door.

KNOCK! KNOCK! KNOCK!

ARE YOU SURE?

I opened the door. Hercule stood in front of me, his paws on his hips.

"What's the matter with you, Geronimo?" he scolded. "Don't you know how to treat a LADY?"

Huh? What was he squeaking about?

"A true gentlemouse would have walked his date home," he explained. "I just left Miss Lovelyfur in front of her cabin after you abandoned her."

Now I was completely confused. I had just said good night to Lily a few minutes ago. . . .

Hercule explained that he was walking back to his cabin when he spotted Lily. She said she had been walking down the stairs to her cabin when she'd SLIPPED and fallen.

"Luckily, she grabbed on to a rope dangling from the Sky Deck. Then I rescued her," Hercule squeaked proudly.

I frowned. Hercule's story didn't make any sense.

"Are you sure it was her?" I squeaked.

"Of course," Hercule insisted. "I even carried her HEAVY backpack. By the way, have you noticed that she has one green eye and one BLUE eye?"

Empress
113

Holey Swiss Cheese!

I closed my eyes and pictured Lily. The first day I met her, her eyes had been clear BLUE, like a summer sky. But then at the awards ceremony, her eyes were the color of sparkling green emeralds. What was going on?

Later that night, we gathered in Thea's cabin to see if we could solve the mystery.

"When Count Richpaws was meeting with the captain, we checked out his cabin," Benjamin said. "We found a ROPE tied outside his window, and a

BLUE contact lens on the floor."

"Just like the contact I found on the floor in the countess's cabin!" Bugsy exclaimed.

Two different-colored eyes? A blue contact lens?

"**Holey Swiss cheese!**" I squeaked. "I think I've figured it out!"

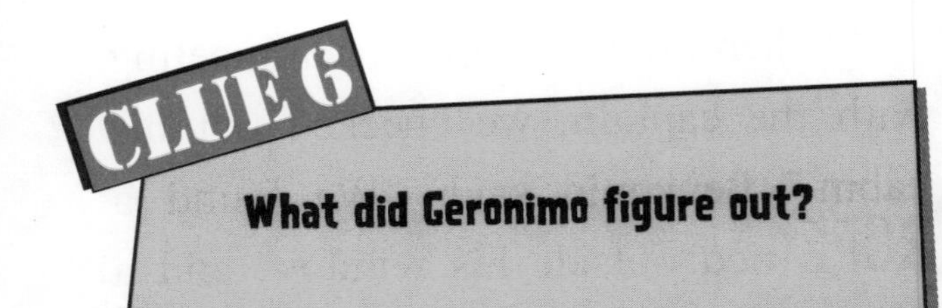

To Catch a Thief

After I explained my suspicions to everyone, Hercule came up with a plan to catch the THIEF. Too bad it involved little old me. I was a nervous wreck!

The next day, we set the plan in motion. First, I invited Miss Lovelyfur to lunch. Then I told her

about my precious CHEESE RIND collection from the 1700s.

"I always carry it with me," I explained. "It's too VALUABLE to leave at home. I hid it in my cabin. I just hope it's safe with all of these THEFTS!"

Lily's blue eyes FLASHED with excitement. "Oh, I'm sure it's safe," she said soothingly.

The Trap

That **evening**, everyone on the ship gathered in the ballroom. The captain announced a big **SURPRISE**.

"One of our passengers has decided to put up a very PRECIOUS object for auction," he said. "The proceeds will go to benefit needy mice in New Mouse City!"

"A PRECIOUS object . . . How interesting," Miss Lovelyfur commented. "I wonder what it is. And who could the passenger be?"

I smiled at her. "It's me!" I said.

"You remember my CHEESE collection?" I explained. "Well, I decided to donate it for a good cause."

At my news, Lily's fur turned as pale as a slice of mozzarella. Suddenly, she headed for the door.

"Be right back," she mumbled.

But she didn't get far. Just then, Benjamin, Bugsy, Thea, and Hercule arrived. Hercule was escorting a mouse who looked EXACTLY like Lily! Yep, the two mice were identical except for one thing: the Lily standing next to me had BLUE eyes. And the Lily with Hercule had green eyes!

Twin Thieves

"**WHAT IS GOING ON HERE?!**" the captain demanded.

"Well, Captain," Hercule squeaked, "you don't have to worry about any more thefts, because here is your thief. Well, actually your **two** thieves."

I was about to confront the Lily beside me, but I never got the chance. Two seconds later, she

Two thieves?!

It turned out that the thieves were actually twins named Samantha and Sasha Stickypaws. They had used colored contact lenses to trick everyone on the ship into thinking they were one mouse.

Samantha was a registered passenger, but Sasha had snuck aboard the ship.

During the day, the two mice dressed alike so that they could walk around the boat at the same time. While Samantha looked for rich passengers on

the **POOL** deck, Sasha searched the cabins below.

At night, one sister **broke** into the cabins, stealing PRECIOUS items. Meanwhile, the other sister made sure

everyone saw her dining and dancing with me so no one would **suspect** her.

When Hercule was done explaining everything, I felt a little FOOLISH. After all, the Stickypaws twins had set me up! I should have known there was something STRANGE about Lily Lovelyfur. Right then and there, I promised myself I'd never again get sidetracked by an interesting female rodent. But that got me thinking about Petunia Pretty Paws. She was kind, smart, and completely fascinating. I sighed. Something told me I might have a little trouble keeping that promise.

SMOOTH SAILING!

I was still thinking about Petunia as I watched the Stickypaws twins being led away. Of course, the captain had them return all of the PRECIOUS objects they had stolen.

Count Richie Richpaws apologized to Thea for accusing her of stealing his gold watch collection. Then he decided to give the whole collection away in the charity auction. Soon, lots of other passengers decided to donate items to the auction. It was an enormouse success!

I was so happy we were making money for my favorite charity, I almost forgot all about the THIEVES and my seasickness. In fact, I had a feeling that the rest of the cruise would be . . .

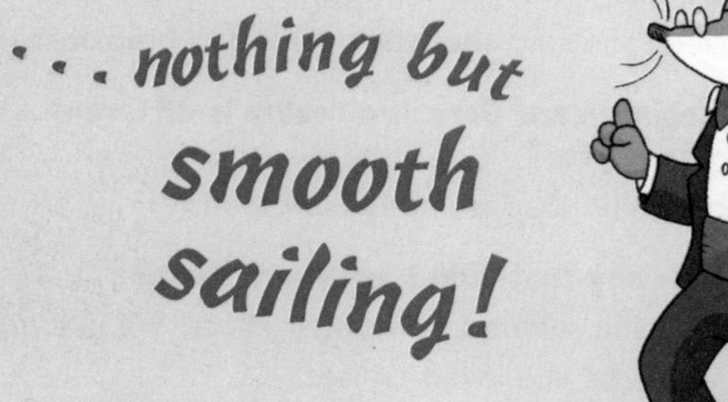

1 **Look at the illustration on page thirty. Can you spot something odd in Lily Lovelyfur's cabin?**
There is a shadow on the wall that's not from Lily.

2 **What do we know now about the mysterious thief?**
That he/she wears contact lenses.

3 **What did Geronimo Stilton see that was so strange?**
He saw Miss Lovelyfur appear in different places at almost the same time. First she said she was going to the pool, then she said she was heading to breakfast.

4 **What do Benjamin and Geronimo realize is different about Lily Lovelyfur?**
Her eye color changed from blue to green.

5 **What did Lily say that didn't make any sense?**
She said that she suffered from seasickness. But in the morning, she said she loved cruises.

6 **What did Geronimo figure out?**
That the blue contact lenses found in the two cabins explained the different color of Lily's eyes. They also proved she had been in both the countess's and the count's cabins.

HOW MANY QUESTIONS DID YOU ANSWER CORRECTLY?

ALL 6 CORRECT: You are a **SUPER-SQUEAKY INVESTIGATOR!**

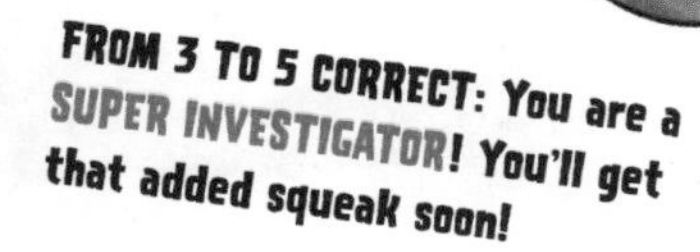

FROM 3 TO 5 CORRECT: You are a **SUPER INVESTIGATOR!** You'll get that added squeak soon!

LESS THAN 3 CORRECT: You are a **GOOD INVESTIGATOR!** Keep practicing to get super-squeaky!

Farewell until the next mystery!

Geronimo Stilton

Check out all my mini-mysteries!

Geronimo Stilton
THE SUPER SCAM
MINI MYSTERY 1

THE LAKE MONSTER
MINI MYSTERY 2

Geronimo Stilton
THE MOUSE HOAX

Geronimo Stilton
THE CAT GANG
SCHOLASTIC
MINI MYSTERY 4

Geronimo Stilton
THE DOUBLE CROSS
SCHOLASTIC
MINI MYSTERY 5

Be sure to read all my fabumouse adventures!

#1 Lost Treasure of the Emerald Eye

#2 The Curse of the Cheese Pyramid

#3 Cat and Mouse in a Haunted House

#4 I'm Too Fond of My Fur!

#5 Four Mice Deep in the Jungle

#6 Paws Off, Cheddarface!

#7 Red Pizzas for a Blue Count

#8 Attack of the Bandit Cats

#9 A Fabumouse Vacation for Geronimo

#10 All Because of a Cup of Coffee

#11 It's Halloween, You 'Fraidy Mouse!

#12 Merry Christmas, Geronimo!

#13 The Phantom of the Subway

#14 The Temple of the Ruby of Fire

#15 The Mona Mousa Code

#16 A Cheese-Colored Camper

#17 Watch Your Whiskers, Stilton!

#18 Shipwreck on the Pirate Islands

#19 My Name Is Stilton, Geronimo Stilton

#20 Surf's Up, Geronimo!

#21 The Wild, Wild West

#22 The Secret of Cacklefur Castle

A Christmas Tale

#23 Valentine's Day Disaster

#24 Field Trip to Niagara Falls

#25 The Search for Sunken Treasure

#26 The Mummy with No Name

#27 The Christmas Toy Factory

#28 Wedding Crasher

#29 Down and Out Down Under

#30 The Mouse Island Marathon

#31 The Mysterious Cheese Thief

Christmas Catastrophe

#32 Valley of the Giant Skeletons

#33 Geronimo and the Gold Medal Mystery

#34 Geronimo Stilton, Secret Agent

#35 A Very Merry Christmas

#36 Geronimo's Valentine

#37 The Race Across America

#38 A Fabumouse School Adventure

#39 Singing Sensation

#40 The Karate Mouse

#41 Mighty Mount Kilimanjaro

#42 The Peculiar Pumpkin Thief

#43 I'm Not a Supermouse!

#44 The Giant Diamond Robbery

#45 Save the White Whale!

#46 The Haunted Castle

#47 Run for the Hills, Geronimo!

#48 The Mystery in Venice

#49 The Way of the Samurai

#50 This Hotel Is Haunted

#51 The Enormouse Pearl Heist

#52 Mouse in Space!

#53 Rumble in the Jungle

#54 Get into Gear, Stilton!

#55 The Golden Statue Plot

#56 Flight of the Red Bandit

The Hunt for the Golden Book

#57 The Stinky Cheese Vacation

#58 The Super Chef Contest

Don't miss my journey through time!

About the Author

Born in New Mouse City, Mouse Island, **Geronimo Stilton** is Rattus Emeritus of Mousomorphic Literature and of Neo-Ratonic Comparative Philosophy. For the past twenty years, he has been running *The Rodent's Gazette*, New Mouse City's most widely read daily newspaper.

Stilton was awarded the Ratitzer Prize for his scoops on *The Curse of the Cheese Pyramid* and *The Search for Sunken Treasure*. He has also received the Andersen 2000 Prize for Personality of the Year. One of his bestsellers won the 2002 eBook Award for world's best ratlings' electronic book. His works have been published all over the globe.

In his spare time, Mr. Stilton collects antique cheese rinds and plays golf. But what he most enjoys is telling stories to his nephew Benjamin.

6
5
4
1
3
2
. Main entrance
. Printing presses (where the books and newspaper are printed)
. Accounts department
. Editorial room (where the editors, illustrators, and designers work)
. Geronimo Stilton's office
. Helicopter landing pad
THE RODENT'S GAZETTE

1
9
4
8
2
18
3
32
RODENT
RIVER
11
13
12
10
19
46
45
17
22
15
5
7
20
26
28
40
14
16
25
36
23
24
27
21
38
33
37
29
44
Beach
31
30
41
6
34
42
39
35
43

Map of New Mouse City

1. Industrial Zone
2. Cheese Factories
3. Angorat International Airport
4. WRAT Radio and Television Station
5. Cheese Market
6. Fish Market
7. Town Hall
8. Snotnose Castle
9. The Seven Hills of Mouse Island
10. Mouse Central Station
11. Trade Center
12. Movie Theater
13. Gym
14. Catnegie Hall
15. Singing Stone Plaza
16. The Gouda Theater
17. Grand Hotel
18. Mouse General Hospital
19. Botanical Gardens
20. Cheap Junk for Less (Trap's store)
21. Parking Lot
22. Mouseum of Modern Art
23. University and Library
24. *The Daily Rat*
25. *The Rodent's Gazette*
26. Trap's House
27. Fashion District
28. The Mouse House Restaurant
29. Environmental Protection Center
30. Harbor Office
31. Mousidon Square Garden
32. Golf Course
33. Swimming Pool
34. Blushing Meadow Tennis Courts
35. Curlyfur Island Amusement Park
36. Geronimo's House
37. Historic District
38. Public Library
39. Shipyard
40. Thea's House
41. New Mouse Harbor
42. Luna Lighthouse
43. The Statue of Liberty
44. Hercule Poirat's Office
45. Petunia Pretty Paws's House
46. Grandfather William's House

This way to the Rodent Straits
Brigand's Isle
Tomcat Island
Pirate Ship of Cats
Hamster Islands
Blue Dolphin Bay
Coral Reefs
This way to the Mousific Ocean
Stray Cat Harbor
Cat's Claw Bay
Panther Archipelago
Swissville
Cheddarton
Mouseport
San Mouscisco
This way to the Ratlantic Ocean
New Mouse City
Mousefort Beach
Furflung Island
N
W
E
S
MOUSE ISLAND
This way to the Sea of Mice
1
2
3
4
5
6
7
8
9
10
11
12
13
14
15
16
17
18
19
20
21
22
23
24
25
26
27
28
29
30
31
32
33
34
35
36
37

Map of Mouse Island

1. Big Ice Lake
2. Frozen Fur Peak
3. Slipperyslopes Glacier
4. Coldcreeps Peak
5. Ratzikistan
6. Transratania
7. Mount Vamp
8. Roastedrat Volcano
9. Brimstone Lake
10. Poopedcat Pass
11. Stinko Peak
12. Dark Forest
13. Vain Vampires Valley
14. Goose Bumps Gorge
15. The Shadow Line Pass
16. Penny Pincher Castle
17. Nature Reserve Park
18. Las Ratayas Marinas
19. Fossil Forest
20. Lake Lake
21. Lake Lakelake
22. Lake Lakelakelake
23. Cheddar Crag
24. Cannycat Castle
25. Valley of the Giant Sequoia
26. Cheddar Springs
27. Sulfurous Swamp
28. Old Reliable Geyser
29. Vole Vale
30. Ravingrat Ravine
31. Gnat Marshes
32. Munster Highlands
33. Mousehara Desert
34. Oasis of the Sweaty Camel
35. Cabbagehead Hill
36. Rattytrap Jungle
37. Rio Mosquito

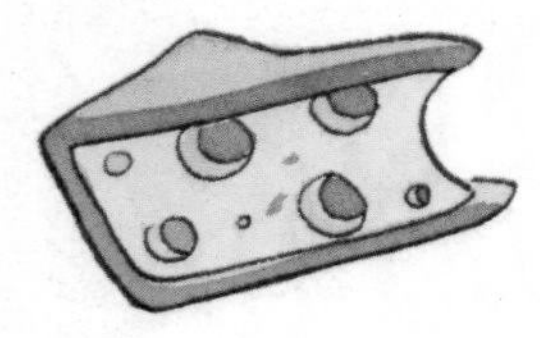

Dear mouse friends,
Thanks for reading, and farewell
until the next mystery!

Geronimo Stilton